Linda Loveridge was born in the Midlands. She has four children who grew up listening to her made-up stories. She moved to Florida where she became a manager of a bookstore. Combining her love for nature, animals, magic and storytelling, she began to write. After fourteen years she moved back to the UK and retired to Leicestershire in her cottage in the countryside. Linda has various diplomas in holistic therapy but after her son died she concentrated mostly on her writing.

To all my children: Miranda, Rick and Temica.

In memory of my son, Lee, who couldn't live in this world but now lives in Chittle Bit Lilly.

Linda Loveridge

CHITTLE BIT LILLY

AUSTIN MACAULEY PUBLISHERS™

LONDON • CAMBRIDGE • NEW YORK • SHARJAH

A CIP catalogue record for this title is available from the British Library.

ISBN 9781398405783 (Paperback)
ISBN 9781398424166 (ePub e-book)

www.austinmacauley.com

First Published (2021)
Austin Macauley Publishers Ltd
25 Canada Square
Canary Wharf
London
E14 5LQ

Table of Contents

Synopsis

Chittle Bit Lilly (spoonerism) is an upside-down (wrong-way-around) village, where the inhabitants sleep during the day and stay awake at night.

Lee, a human, lives in Chittle Bit Lilly, along with his friends the animal warriors.

They are protected by a magical dome that hides them from the outside world.

They go out into this world at night and clean up the environment.

The village thrives on kindness, love, friendship and respect.

The animal warriors are: the babbities, the wirrels, the spindlers, the bidgebodgers, the sneasles, the squeakers, the twitterflys, the fledgehoggles and the hodgers.

Chapter 1
In the Beginning

Chittle Bit Lilly was an upside-down, wrong-way-around village, whose residents were all very unusual animals, except for Lee.

Lee was a human, a man, a kind man who looked after all the animals and they looked after him.

The village square was actually a star, which shone during the day. It was the most magical and wondrous star and as soon as the sun rose, everyone congregated in the centre of the village and replenished their energies by lying on the star and soaking up the magic rays. The babbities, the sneasles, the fledgehoggles, the wirrels, the squeakers, the twitterflys, the hodgers, the spindlers and the bidgebodgers, every last one of them, came.

Lee organized the area, making sure everyone was present and inside the star before they all settled down to sleep.

Around the borders of Chittle Bit Lilly was a magical dome that protected them from the outside world. It glowed a bright blue when activated and no one in the outside world could see it.

When the darkness came, they all woke up equipped with magical powers.

They could all see very well in the dark, hear at long distances and grow double in size, among other things.

They were the animal warriors!

Their main mission was to clean up the environment beyond their village.

The outside world was filled with utoas: human-shaped hazy blobs that the warriors called hazers.

The hazers didn't really see the animal warriors, which was how they liked it.

Now and then they would be confronted by a hazer but the sneasles soon take care of that.

Art and Choo were sneasles and they acted as agents for the warriors. They were chosen as agents because they were cunning and could outwit the hazers every time, or so they thought.

The babbities could jump extremely high, allowing them to clean rubbish from rooftops or trees. They also stamped their feet loudly, which warned the warriors to be extra careful and more aware of their surroundings.

The night in the outside world was alive with many other creatures, and on occasion, they had been known to assist the warriors, foxes, deer, bats and even cats if need be.

Not all of the outside-world animals were friendly, though, so the sooner they cleared the rubbish, the better, as their time in this other world was limited.

The warriors were very grateful for all the help they would get and often made friends with many outside-world animals.

The fledgehoggles had long noses and long spines all over. Their bodies could spin and roll, quickly picking up debris as they went.

It truly was a magical sight to see. Oh, did I tell you they were ginger!

The net weavers or spindlers spun nets to collect the rubbish. These nets were extremely strong and could hold huge amounts of waste.

Once the nets had been made, along came the wirrels, who held the edges of the net in their paws, and like fishermen, gathered the rubbish in the nets, ready to take back to Chittle Bit Lilly.

There were many squeakers who lived in Chittle Bit Lilly but the bravest of all were Itty, Bitty and Boo.

Squeakers were so adept at gnawing that their teeth could tear through anything, be it wire, plastic, rope, etc., and would often be seen releasing trapped animals that had been caught by the hazers.

The hodgers ate anything left over by the hazers. They had a shovel-shaped nose and mouth to scoop up the food. If they didn't eat it all, they would find a compost mound and deposit it there.

The twitterflys were the look-outs. They would go through the protective energy field first to make sure things were safe for the rest of the warriors. They were also the last to return, sometimes with gifts collected by the outside animals for Lee.

After the warriors gathered all of the rubbish from the outside world for the night, they brought it into Chittle Bit Lilly, where it all instantly disappeared.

That is why Chittle Bit Lilly was always clean and tidy.

Lee was a very, very kind utoa who preferred the company of animals. He had lived in Chittle Bit Lilly for many years and enjoyed living with the warriors so much that he never left the village.

Lee was the only one that could open the protective power around the village. He also closed it when the mission for the night was done.

He did this with kindness!

Chittle Bit Lilly was a beautiful place to live, with enchanted forests, fresh clear running streams and deep valleys. It was so magical that the flowers never died.

Everyone loved living here and was so happy.

When you walked around, you saw a large old brick house, the only one in the village.

The squeakers lived there.

They needed a big house because there were so many of them. Squeakers were very tiny yellow creatures that possessed very long sharp teeth, very much like a vampire. They could be quite intimidating when all together, but also looked extremely funny scurrying everywhere.

Now, the babbities lived in lush green mounds and on top of the mounds grew the babbities favourite food...

Lollipops! They adored lollipops. Babbities had small pointed ears, like a cat, and large back legs. They were dark blue with a light blue stubby tail.

The wirrels and hodgers lived underground and built tunnels which joined up in the middle.

Wirrels were small and white with a brush for their tail.

This they used to sweep up after a night's cleaning venture.

Hodgers were green and, with their shovel-shaped noses, could easily dig their tunnels but often got stuck because of their fat bellies.

The fledgehoggles lived in trees. You had to be very aware when walking underneath trees in case there was a sleeping fledgehoggle. They often fell off branches and those spines could get everywhere, ouch!

There were numerous brightly coloured sheds dotted around the village, which were the homes of the bidgebodgers. They loved bright colours. You couldn't stand still or they would paint you a bright colour too!

Bidgebodgers were very strong and had large finger-like paws. On their paws were bright colours which looked like nail varnish.

No, they didn't paint them, they were born that way. If you saw a tree-house high up you would find the twitterflys. They had rope bridges hanging from tree to tree for visiting guests.

They were completely black with small bodies and large wings. When they got excited their feathers glowed purple.

They looked so clumsy on the ground, but when they flew it was an awesome sight.

Now the spindlers…

Well, they bunked anywhere. They were bright red, with a suction cup on their butts, which is where the nets came from. The suction cup was small but they could easily sit on the cup and take a rest. It looked so funny especially when they were all together because their long legs dangled freely when they sat.

The agents for the warriors were the sneasles, they also lived all over.

Anywhere they could sleep for the day or enjoy a meal, they would be seen.

I did tell you they were cunning and cheeky, with their flat cap hairstyle and grey suit look, but they were also delightful little monsters.

Lee lived in a beautiful house made of wood. It was built around two very large trees: one in the kitchen and the other in the bedroom. All the warriors helped Lee build it and he loved it! It was nestled in the middle of a wood which was surrounded by beautiful flowers.

Most of his visitors climbed down the trunks of the trees and when they did, there was always a chance for a party.

Lee was always content and very happy, until one night when he seemed sad and distant with the animals.

He was different.

Chapter 2

The Mission

'What are we going to do?' said Babs the babbitie.

'Ssshh… he's coming,' replied Wes the wirrel.

'What are you all up to?' asked Lee while looking at the warriors.

'Waiting for you,' they all replied.

The warriors were so worried about Lee because he was never sad or unhappy, but he was now!

All the warriors gathered around the star chattering and discussing Lee, waiting for the sun to rise so they could settle down on the star and sleep.

It was a magical sight as all the warriors, including Lee, found their place in the centre of the star and lay down.

As soon as one closed their eyes and drifted off to sleep, his or her body glowed blue as the magical energy swirled around them, renewing their powers.

Chittle Bit Lilly comes to life at night mainly because of the warriors, but also because it was an upside-down world with special magic day and night.

The village was set in between two valleys and surrounded by woodland.

Many of the outside animals had heard of Chittle Bit Lilly and told the most exciting tales of the warriors and Lee. Most would love to be able to see it and even visit one day.

The moon was now full. Its white light awoke the warriors. One by one they prepared for the night's mission once awakened, growing in size.

Their mission was slightly different tonight as they needed to find a solution to help Lee.

When they returned after cleaning up all the mess the hazers had left behind, they decided to hold a meeting to discuss what they would do about Lee.

'Don't forget the meeting,' whispered Babs, as all the warriors passed by her to get to the door of the dome.

They all acknowledged her in their own way.

Lee prepared himself to open the door but didn't seem able to do it.

The warriors waited patiently as he tried again.

'It's not opening,' snorted Hog, one of the hodgers.

'What's wrong?'

'I don't know,' replied Lee, very frustrated.

'Where has your kindness gone?' asked Babs.

'It's still there. I'll try again,' he sighed.

After gathering all the kindness he had inside of him, he lifted his right hand and directed the door to open. Thankfully, this time it did, allowing the warriors to squeeze through, followed by the remaining twitterflys.

Little, the largest of the fledgehoggles (of course the other warriors thought that name was very appropriate), signalled Lee to close the door as he was the last to go through.

'You're supposed to go through last, Little,' one of the twitterflys said.

'We can't do everything,' came the reply.

'Let's get this sorted a little quicker tonight so we can have our meeting,' Choo, one of the sneasles, spoke.

They proceeded to scout the area to see the damage. 'It doesn't seem too bad,' Wes said. 'Maybe the hazers are starting to clean this place up.'

'Yeah, right!' came the reply.

'I don't think so,' a hodger whizzed by scooping up some leftovers. 'Yummy,' he giggled. The spindlers got to work spinning their net, while the wirrels collected all the rubbish that was left.

During the night the warriors wondered how they were going to complete their mission when they didn't even know what was troubling Lee.

'Stay completely still,' demanded Siggy, one of the spindlers. 'Look,' she said, flicking her head sideways.

Everyone turned around and noticed a hazer staring at them.

'She can see us,' Itty, one of the squeakers, spoke.

'Whoops.' Sure enough, a young girl was watching the warriors and seemed to be able to see all of them.

The silence lasted for a few minutes as they looked at the girl and she looked at them.

She was a pretty girl, with dark hair, lovely green eyes and the kindest of faces.

Suddenly, one of the young fledgehoggles bolted and landed right at the girl's feet.

'Whoops,' she laughed.

'And who are you?'

The fledgehoggle was so startled he shook all the rubbish from his spines, making it fly everywhere.

All the warriors laughed and giggled.

The girl spluttered, fanning away the mess that had now settled on her.

'Who are you?' she asked again.

'I'm Miranda.'

It took a few seconds but Babs answered. 'Do not give us away. We are the animal warriors, we clean up this place at night while you lot are sleeping.'

The girl replied, 'I would never do that. Thanks for cleaning up the mess. Some people are really dirty.'

'How come you can see us?' asked Choo.

'I really don't know,' she answered. 'I have lost one of my puppies and came out to find her.'

'Whereabouts did you lose her?' Wes questioned her.

'That's just it, I don't know, she just ran out of the back door, never to be seen again.'

'We have to go now,' Babs interrupted. 'If you come back here tomorrow night, we will help you find your puppy.'

'Really… would you? That's so kind of you!' she replied.

They all said goodbye and planned to meet up the next night.

The warriors made their way to the door of the dome. It was a small entrance surrounded by ivy, which trailed over and around an oak door.

It looked too small to allow the warriors through, but remember Chittle Bit Lilly was a magical village so anything was possible.

The hazers couldn't see the entrance so it was easy for the warriors to suddenly disappear.

On the way they discussed how they were going to have their meeting without Lee knowing.

The twitterfly and the bidgebodgers were always the last to go through. The twitterfly were the look-out so it seemed right that they should go last.

And the bidgebodgers, well, they were just lazy!

As they waited for everyone to go in, they observed how the rubbish instantly disappeared when they entered and they shrunk back to their normal size.

Lee was there to greet them. He was always there to greet them and the warriors were very grateful for that.

It was still night but the sun was going to be rising soon. 'Well I'm going straight home for a while,' Lee muttered with his head bowed. 'I'll see you shortly when the sun comes up.'

'OK,' replied Babs immediately, looking at the warriors, who all smiled.

Meeting, they all thought.

Chapter 3

The Meeting

All the babbities were there. So were the two twitterflys Swoop and Joop.

The wirrels, Wes and the gang, sat next to Siggy and the spindlers (sounds like a band).

Boring, Snoring and the rest of the bidgebodgers were there too.

Art and Choo, the only sneasles in Chittle Bit Lilly, organised the seating for the warriors. Some were not happy.

'Sit down,' shouted Art.

'Who's he think he is,' Little piped up, shoving Hog further along the log they were sitting on. Bog, another hodger, giggled.

Itty, Bitty, Boo and the rest of the squeakers squeaked so loudly that Babs had to call for order.

'Order,' she shouted, stamping her right foot. As she did so, blue light shot out from under her foot and everything went quiet.

'We must try to keep the noise down,' Babs lowered her voice. 'This meeting is supposed to be a secret.'

'Right,' Choo began, 'who knows why we are here?'

'Oh, sit down Choo, we all know why,' Siggy sighed. The rest of the warriors laughed and then Swoop the twitterfly began.

'What do you think is wrong?' he asked.

Twitterflys were an amazing black colour that glowed purple when they were excited. They loved being friends with cats whenever they could, especially black ones.

Their bodies were small but their wings were huge.

Who knows how they flew. It was magic!

Swoop and Joop were the only twitterflys who lived in Chittle Bit Lilly, which was no problem since they were excellent look-outs.

'Well, I'm wondering if he's lonely,' Babs answered Swoop.

'How can he be lonely? He has us!' Little replied.

'Yes, he does, but he is on his own while we go to the outside world,' Wes explained.

'Perhaps he needs to be with his own kind, the hazers,' Choo commented.

'We… are his own kind,' said Joop.

'Or we need to bring one here to Chittle Bit Lilly,' Hog snorted.

'No way!' the rest of the warriors shouted.

By now, Boring was yawning and Snoring was snoring and they both jumped from their sleep, dazed and confused.

'Keep your voices down,' Babs whispered as Boring and Snoring took note of what was being said at the meeting.

'OK,' yawned Boring. Snoring just grunted.

'Right. Anyone else have any suggestions?' Babs asked. No comments came.

'What we will do then is, tomorrow when we wake up, we'll sit with him and ask a few questions to see if we can find out what he's thinking,' Babs decided.

'Good idea,' Wes replied.

Art and Choo rallied them around, urging everyone to make their way to the star to sleep.

Lee was already there laying on the star, preparing to renew his magic.

Tomorrow came quickly, only it was night-time for the warriors. They all woke up with the moon and slowly began to get ready for the outside world.

Babs was sitting with Lee. 'Do you get lonely when we are gone?' she asked him.

'No, not really. I miss you all but I have things to do,' Lee answered.

'Would you like to come with us? someone else asked.

'Of course not. The outside world is not for me. I love Chittle Bit Lilly. Why all the questions?' Lee frowned.

'Oh, no reason. Have a lovely night, we'll see you soon,' Babs smiled.

Babs and Wes joined the other warriors and waited as Lee opened the door to the dome.

They were gone!

That night they met up with Miranda who was now frantic with worry. She had brought her little sister, Temica, with her.

Temica had big brown eyes, freckles and the cutest of faces.

'I still haven't found my puppy, she must be starving,' Miranda started to cry.

Temica held her hand and told Miranda it would be fine.

'It's OK, we will stop cleaning up for the night and look for your puppy,' Babs comforted her.

So they all did just that! Everyone was on look-out this night.

They searched under hedges, in abandoned houses, under treetops, under cars, everywhere they could think of, even on the rooftops. Babbities are great at jumping very high but... they found nothing. 'Well we have searched everywhere,' Siggy said.

'It's getting late,' Babs stated. 'We must return.'

Miranda became very upset. 'Don't give up, Miranda,' Babs comforted her, 'we will be back tomorrow. Gods are very strong.'

'Gods?' Temica seemed puzzled.

'Oh, sorry... dogs to you,' Wes said.

'You call them "gods", why?' asked Miranda.

Just then a fox called Fergus came out from the bushes and spoke.

'Because they are amazingly kind, they are loyal, very loyal, and will do anything for you. Their greatest quality is love. They can also heal you just by being by your side.'

As Fergus finished his speech, Babs had a strange look on her face, she was frowning and her lips were pressed together.

'Mmmmm,' she muttered. 'Hello Fergus, how are you?'

'What's going on?' he asked.

'Miranda has lost her puppy; we've been helping her find her.'

Fergus was a typical orange coloured fox with a bushy tail and black paws. He was the friendliest of foxes, helping the warriors whenever he could.

'We have to go now,' Babs said. 'We will be back tomorrow.'

'I'll be here tomorrow,' said Fergus.

'Thank you,' Miranda waved goodbye to them all.

'Thanks,' Temica said. 'Will see you tomorrow.'

The warriors slowly made their way back to Chittle Bit Lilly.

'Do you think we will find her?' Miranda asked looking at Fergus.

'I'm sure we will,' Fergus replied. 'I know many hiding places.'

'Thanks so much,' she said while hugging Fergus.

'Watch the fur!' Fergus stepped back.

He wasn't used to hazers hugging him.

'See you tomorrow, then,' Miranda whispered and disappeared up the road with Temica following behind.

Fergus decided he would go to the nearest hiding place before travelling any further.

Chapter 4

Buzzle Joins the Family

'I've got to get there,' panted a little bee.

He lived in the outside world and had heard all about Chittle Bit Lilly.

He was a solitary bee. They usually lived alone, not producing honey like the other bees. It was only that this little bee had started to make honey. The other bees didn't want him near them, so he wanted to find Chittle Bit Lilly and live there.

He had already travelled two miles; that was an awful long way for a bee to fly, especially a little one.

He was about three miles away from the entrance of Chittle Bit Lilly and all he could think about was the magic and the kindness others had told him this place had.

Just keep going, he thought to himself. *Just keep going.*

On and on he buzzed, not even sure if he was close to Chittle Bit Lilly, although he could feel it inside of him, the magic.

Then he saw the warriors ahead. They all had magical hearing and heard the buzzing from far away.

'What's that buzzing?' Itty, one of the squeakers, asked.

'Yes I can hear it too!' said Babs.

Suddenly the bee came into view about half a mile ahead. He became so excited that he pushed harder and one of his wings began to tear. This put him off balance. He spun and swerved and then landed headfirst in a nearby puddle.

The warriors rushed to help him.

'It's a buzzle,' Wes said while looking closely at the little bee. 'He's really hurt.'

Siggy, one of the spindlers, allowed Wes to slowly place the bee on her back.

They all slowly headed towards the entrance of Chittle Bit Lilly, making sure the little buzzle stayed on Siggy's back.

Lee was at the entrance waiting for them. He waved his hand for the door to open.

He noticed the buzzle.

'Oh, no, what's happened?' he asked.

'Don't know, we just found him in a puddle,' came the reply.

Lee closed the door of the dome, then went straight over to Siggy, who still had the buzzle on her back.

'Is he dead?' asked Little, the largest fledgehoggle.

'Little… be quiet,' Lee ordered. 'C'mon Siggy, follow me to my home, he can stay there until he gets well.'

Lee made a small bed for the bee as soon as they got to his home.

'When the sun comes up, I will take him to the star, he will be healed there,' Lee told the warriors.

Lee kept a close eye on the bee and hoped he and the warriors could help him.

The sun started to rise so one by one the warriors lay down in the centre of the star.

Lee placed the little bed with the sleeping bee inside next to him, hoping that the magic would heal him.

As they all slept the magic did its work. Bit by bit the tiny wing that shone brightly started to repair itself. The blue energy entered the bee, filling his little body so much that it lifted him off the bed while he slept. Every now and then you could hear a slight buzz as the energy flowed through him.

It was time to wake as the sun set and darkness took hold. Everyone was ready for the little bee. He was still sleeping.

'Look,' said Babs, 'his wing is back to normal.'

'I wish he would wake up,' Boo, one of the squeakers, squeaked.

'He will, eventually,' Lee smiled.

'But he must be exhausted.'

Before the warriors went to the outside world, Lee started to walk towards his house. 'I will look after him at my house,' he said.

'Let's call him Buzzle,' Hog suggested.

'Wait until he wakes up, then we can initiate him,' Lee said.

'Oh yeah, I forget about that,' said Little.

The warriors prepared themselves for the outside world and waited patiently by the door, discussing the little bee.

'I hope he recovers,' Babs said.

'He will,' Wes replied.

All the warriors were eager for the bee to stay and became very excited.

Lee came back and opened the door to the outside world and the warriors marched through. Then off he went back to his house, walking slowly, thinking about the little bee.

Lee's house was simply called "Lee's cottage". It was the most beautiful, comfortable cottage in Chittle Bit Lilly.

All of the furniture was made from wood. The wood came from the surrounding trees. All the warriors worked really hard finding branches on the floor or cutting them down if they were no longer good for the tree.

While out cleaning the outside world, the warriors had found some wood from the trees in one of the fields and brought it back for Lee to use.

His settee was covered in wool, so snuggly and warm.

Everyone loved to visit!

The bee slept most of the night, while Lee sat beside him on a chair. His wing was fully healed and the bee seemed back to normal.

Lee thought how wonderful it was to have a buzzle at Chittle Bit Lilly, hoping that the little bee would stay.

Suddenly, the bee grew twice his normal size and then shrunk back again. Lee laughed and thought, *he has magic! We must do the initiation straight away.* Then it happened. The bee slowly looked around the room, then smiled at Lee.

'Am I in Chittle Bit Lilly?' he asked.

'Yes, you definitely are,' Lee laughed.

The bee turned over onto his feet and twizzled around, buzzing loudly. He then flew straight to Lee, landing on his shoulder.

'So, you are happy then? asked Lee.

'Very, very happy,' the bee replied. 'I want to stay here forever!'

Lee laughed again, carrying the bee on his shoulder to let the warriors back in to Chittle Bit Lilly.

As they all rushed in, there was an enormous cheer when they saw the little bee happy and well again.

Everyone clambered into Lee's home. There was about to be another party.

'I can't believe you are awake and fine,' Babs smiled. The little bee was so excited to see everyone that he grew large again and everyone laughed loudly.

'Right, it's time for your initiation,' Lee said while looking at the bee.

'Will it hurt?' he asked nervously.

'Oh, no one gets hurt here,' Wes said.

All the warriors gathered around and sat patiently, waiting for Lee to begin. 'Little bee,' Lee said, then asked a question. 'If a friend wants help, do you: number one... help them? Number two... get someone else to help them? Or number three... walk away?'

Instantly, the bee said, 'Number one... help them.'

They all cheered!

'You have been initiated!' they shouted. 'You are now a warrior and your name is Buzzle.'

He smiled and was so grateful to be part of this magical family.

Chapter 5

The Nasties

Ferqus came out early. He usually waited for the sun to set before he foraged around but he wanted to look for Miranda's puppy.

He headed to a well-known field where it was easy to hide, there were lots of bushes and small trees ideal to snuggle down under.

Then he saw them!

The Nasties, a gang of slugs, all heading towards the gate.

'What you lot doing?' he snorted.

'Oy!' the leader shouted. 'What's your problem?'

All the slugs moved towards Fergus, poking their antennae in the air and producing so much slime it made Fergus feel sick.

Fergus knew they are up to something and it seemed obvious to him that the puppy must be around somewhere. Slugs could smell quite well and especially if they thought there was food around. He knew he had to get into the field quickly if he had any hope of finding the puppy.

So he made a giant leap over the slugs, over the gate and into the field.

'You can't fool us, foxy, we know you're up to something.' The Nasties continued under the gate and into the field.

There were so many of them, and so much slime, that Fergus couldn't concentrate properly. *What shall I do?* he thought. *I can't continue as they will follow.*

On one side of the field, Fergus could see part of a wired fence coming down, so he headed for that.

It was very dark now and ahead he could hear utoas shouting.

'You, got the torch?' one asked.

'Yep,' came the reply.'

Oh no, he thought, *Nasties on either side. Think, Fergus, think! The slugs I can just about deal with, even though they make me sick, but the utoas? No way.*

He jumped and landed under the nearest hedge, right next to the puppy. The puppy was trapped and the wire of the fence was wrapped around its little paw, cutting into her skin and making it bleed. The puppy wasn't moving but she was still alive.

Fergus lay still as he heard the utoas approaching.

'Can't see anything,' the figure said.

At that point Fergus held his breath so they couldn't hear his breathing. Once they had passed him, he let out all the air, producing a whistle.

Whoops! He thought. *I hope they didn't hear that.*

'What was that, listen,' the other utoa whispered.

He switched on his torch pointing it towards the hedge. By now, Fergus had slowly shuffled further away, carefully dragging the puppy with him.

'There's nothing there,' said a utoa. 'You're just scared of the dark.'

'Eeewww, slugs! Nasty things, loads of 'em,' shouted the utoa.

The Nasties had reached where Fergus and the puppy were but had to wait for the utoas to pass by or else they would have been trodden on.

It looked so funny, the utoas trying to avoid the Nasties.

Fergus thought they were all crazy and wished they would go away.

Eventually, the utoas left the field, leaving the slugs to head under the hedge.

'Not so fast,' said Little the fledgehoggle. 'Slugs are a delicacy and there are none in Chittle Bit Lilly.'

'Oh no,' shouted the Nasties and bundled together, hoping for safety in numbers.

What you saw next were spines, slime and a huge mess.

No more of that, thought Fergus and called for help.

'Right, squeakers, do your best.'

Yes! the warriors had joined Fergus in the field. What a relief.

Itty, Bitty and Boo, three of the squeakers, gnawed at the wire, gently easing the puppy's paw free.

It was still lifeless but Fergus knew it was alive.

The bidgebodgers Boring and Snoring, who were very strong, carried the puppy to the gate and waited for Miranda to come.

Swoop, one of the twitterflys, headed off to find her.

He found her at the door of the dome, looking quite anxious.

'Miranda,' Swoop chattered, 'go home and find something to put your puppy in, we have found her.'

'Oh, thank you,' she sighed, 'I'll fetch my trolley.'

'Put some blankets in, she is badly hurt,' Swoop suggested.

Miranda stopped, her eyes wide and hands to her face.

'She's still alive, so hurry, get your trolley!' Swoop said.

A tear trickled down her face as she thought of the poor puppy.

She knew that she should be brave and disappeared down the road towards her house.

Five minutes later, with her trolley dragging behind her and Temica in tow, she got to the gate of the field. 'Wait for me!' shouted Rikki, Miranda and Temica's little brother, and then came running up to them.

'Finally…' Temica rolled her eyes.

'Always late to the table,' Rikki sighed.

'What does that mean?' Temica asked.

'Oh, just that he is always the last one to know anything,' Miranda answered.

'Isn't that all boys?' Temica commented.

Rikki had blonde hair and blue eyes, with the cheekiest of faces. He was annoying most of the time but adorable too.

'Oh, she looks awful, what shall I do?' cried Miranda as she sobbed.

'Take her home and ask your parents to look after her. She may need to go to a vet,' Wes suggested.

Miranda and the others stood staring, not doing or saying anything.

They watched as the warriors very carefully lifted the puppy into the trolley.

'Miranda,' Babs touched her arm, 'you must go home, show your parents so they can help the puppy.'

Eventually Miranda very slowly made her way towards her home, stopping now and then so she, Temica and Rikki could look at the poor puppy.

'What do we do now?' asked Hog.

'Carry on,' said Babs. 'If Miranda needs us, she knows where we are!'

The rest of the night the warriors couldn't concentrate so they decided to go back to Chittle Bit Lilly earlier than usual.

'Thanks so much for your help, Fergus,' said Babs.

'I was pleased to help,' Fergus replied nodding his head. He then sauntered off into the night.

The warriors reached the entrance to Chittle Bit Lilly and signalled to Lee to open the door of the dome. Everyone slowly entered.

Lee mentioned he was going home to check on Buzzle.

'When will he be ready to join us in the outside world?' asked Choo.

'Soon, very soon,' Lee smiled.

'He seems so much better,' Little remarked looking at Lee, with slime dribbling from his mouth.

'Eeewww, wipe your mouth, Little,' Wes started, 'and keep away from me.'

All the warriors laughed.

'Yes, he does, however I think he'll feel even better when I put my idea in to action,' smiled Babs.

'What you up to now?' the squeakers giggled.

'You'll see,' came the reply.

Chapter 6

The Day the God Came

'It's boring,' yawned Boring.

Boring was a bidgebodger and most of the time he sat around saying how boring everything was and then proceeding to yawn.

Obviously, that was why the warriors called him Boring.

'Boring bidgebodger, what are you doing today?' the squeakers Itty, Bitty and Boo would ask, waiting for the usual reply.

'Nothing, it's Boring,' he would reply.

The squeakers would fall about laughing, then Boring would chase them off.

Snoring the bidgebodger really didn't need any introduction, his name said it all.

What a life they all had in Chittle Bit Lilly. The warriors were so happy.

They often sat together after being in the outside world, having parties. Not for a particular reason, but just because.

Lee would always join them. There would be singing and storytelling, lots of fond memories, lots of laughing. True friendship.

The next night Lee opened the door of the dome with Buzzle perched on his shoulder. 'When can I go with them?' Buzzle buzzed.

'Maybe tomorrow. It's quite dangerous out there, especially if the hazers can see you,' he replied.

'I'll be fine, I promise,' Buzzle pleaded.

'I know,' Lee said. 'Soon.'

Outside of Chittle Bit Lilly stood Miranda, with a trolley, her sister Temica and her brother Rikki.

Inside the trolley was the puppy god.

'Is she…?' asked Babs.

'No,' cried Miranda, 'but my parents want to take her to the vet's, she's not getting any better and still hasn't woken up. You know what will happen if she goes to the vet.'

'Yes, I'm afraid I do,' said Babs.

'Not always,' Temica joined in. 'They may heal her.'

'They may not, either,' Rikki piped up.

'Well I have a great idea,' Babs smiled. 'What if we take her into Chittle Bit Lilly and heal her there? It does mean, though, that you wouldn't see her again.' Miranda looked so sad that Babs thought she was going to refuse the offer. She gave the biggest sigh, biting her lip.

'This is so hard,' Miranda said.

Temica gave her a hug. 'It's for the best,' Rikki said. Wes told Miranda that it was better than taking her to the vet and never coming out again.

'At least this way, your puppy will be really looked after and loved.'

'It will be better for her,' Miranda struggled to get the words out.

'Wait until we have cleared up around here, then you can decide,' Little said.

The warriors continued to clean up the environment while Miranda, Temica and Rikki sat by the trolley, stroking the puppy.

The puppy opened her eyes a little, then closed them, making a small panting noise.

Her paw was still so sore and swollen where the wire had cut through her leg.

Miranda knew she would be better with Lee and the warriors.

Lee's kindness and the magic of Chittle Bit Lilly can heal anyone, she thought, covering the puppy with a blanket.

Temica and Rikki both looked at Miranda, smiling and trying to give her support.

She gathered her strength and decided to tell the warriors to take the puppy.

There was a lot of rubbish around that night so the warriors were very tired when they came back to Miranda.

'So, what have you decided?' asked Babs.

'It would be best for you to take her,' Miranda sighed heavily.

'Wise choice,' Hog spluttered, finishing the last few bits of food in his scoop.

'She will be looked after very well,' Siggy the spindler reassured her.

'Yes, very well,' the warriors agreed.

Taking the puppy in his arms, Boring the bidgebodger stood waiting at the door of Chittle Bit Lilly for Lee to open it.

Snoring stood by him, looking on.

It won't be boring now, he thought. Snoring smiled.

Once they had said goodbye to Miranda, Temica and Rikki, the warriors waved to them and watched as they strolled off slowly. The trolley was trailing behind them. Their heads were bowed; their shoulders slumped. Sad little hazers.

The warriors went inside Chittle Bit Lilly.

Lee's face instantly changed. 'What do we have this time?' he asked.

'This is a puppy god,' the warriors said excitedly.

Babs winked at Wes and he winked back.

'Mission completed,' Babs whispered. 'Lee won't be sad anymore now.'

'You are more cunning than the sneasles,' Wes said smiling. 'Well, that's not hard,' said Babs.

They both laughed.

All this time Babs had wanted the puppy god to be in Chittle Bit Lilly. Of course, to heal her, but also to be with Lee and she got her wish.

The puppy god was jet black and had the cutest face, which made everyone fall in love with her.

Lee felt a special connection with her as he bundled her up in a cuddly blanket and sauntered off to his cottage in the woods, with Buzzle following closely behind.

'So, you think she needs any of my honey?' Buzzle asked.

'That's very kind of you,' Lee smiled. 'Do you have enough?'

'Of course, I like to share, anyway,' came the reply.

Once they reached the cottage, Lee laid the puppy gently on his bed. Immediately she opened her eyes.

'Hi, there,' Lee whispered, 'how are you feeling?'

The puppy became agitated and wriggled out of the blanket. 'Ouch!' she said. 'What, wait… I can talk! I can really talk!' The room became silent. Lee looked at Buzzle and then looked at the puppy, waiting for her to speak again.

'Oh! This is so… cool!' she laughed.

Then they all laughed together.

Buzzle buzzed, dancing in front of the puppy. 'You can have some of my honey too,' he said excitedly.

Slowly Buzzle gave some honey to the puppy and she slurped it up immediately.

'Your paw looks very sore, but it is healing.' Lee said, while checking over the puppy's leg.

'My honey will heal it too,' said Buzzle.

'You have been out of it for a couple of days,' Lee told her. 'You'll be fine once you have eaten.'

'A couple of days, that's a long time, no wonder I'm starving,' the puppy god replied.

So Buzzle and Lee tended to all the puppy's needs very willingly.

Lee explained all about Chittle Bit Lilly. The warriors, the magic, the clean-up, the magical dome and so much more, with Buzzle buzzing in every now and then.

'Can I really stay here?' the puppy asked.

'Of course,' Lee replied. 'Once you have slept in the star at the centre of Chittle Bit Lilly, you will have magic. That means, though, that you won't be able to go back to your friends in the outside world.'

'I don't mind because I really like it here already,' she smiled.

Many days and nights went by and finally it was time for the puppy to sleep in the star.

She proudly ambled by Lee's side as they made their way to the star in the centre of Chittle Bit Lilly.

Already the puppy could feel the magic getting stronger inside of her, she was so excited.

'Are you OK?' Lee asked.

'Yes, yes, I can't wait,' the puppy answered.

The warriors joined them as they lay down to sleep. 'I can feel it and see it,' she yawned while looking at Lee.

Then all was quiet.

The moon shone. It was time for all the warriors to wake.

The first was Lee, followed by Buzzle and then the rest of the animals.

The little puppy was last. They all stood over her, waiting. 'Is it time to get up?' she yawned, rubbed her eyes. 'Why are you all looking at me?'

'You are blue, little one,' Lee said laughing. 'It's the magic.' Sure enough, the puppy had turned blue and the magic was still healing her.

'Do we need to initiate her?' Babs looked at Lee.

'Only to give her a name,' Lee replied.

'Can we have a naming party?' Wes asked.

'OK,' Lee laughed, 'let's do it later.'

'What are we going to call her?' Itty, Bitty and Boo squeaked together.

'I will tell you tomorrow, after you have all come back from the outside world.'

Night still had its hold on Chittle Bit Lilly and all the warriors had returned from cleaning up all the hazers' mess.

Everyone congregated around a beautiful open fire outside the squeakers' house.

'Come on now,' Art and Choo, the sneasles, ordered.

'Yippee, a naming party!' Little began to spin.

'Watch out,' said Boring, 'you nearly knocked me over.'

They had a small ceremony where Lee said a few words, welcoming the puppy to Chittle Bit Lilly.

The puppy was right by Lee's side and so happy to be there. He held her in his arms, lifted her high above his head and declared her name to be Ember.

There was so much cheering and laughing as they all welcomed Ember to her new home.

Chapter 7

Gypsy

Everyone had just woken up to see a full moon shining right in the centre of Chittle Bit Lilly.

'Time to clean up the hazers' mess again,' Babs yawned.

'Yep, it's never-ending,' Wes piped up.

'It's for the better, though,' Choo said, convincing himself. 'It helps all the outside animals too.'

'Yes, very much,' Art agreed.

'I just wish the hazers would see that,' Babs sighed.

Ember woke too. Off she went running around chasing everyone, then rolled over in all the grass.

'I love it here, I love it so much,' she said excitedly.

'C'mon, little Ember,' Lee stroked her lovingly, 'we'll walk around Chittle Bit Lilly and check everyone's homes.'

'Where's Buzzle?' asked Little.

'I am here. Waiting to go with you. I am a warrior now,' he buzzed.

'Lee, Lee… wait!' shouted Little.

'What?' came the reply. Lee had just managed to hear Little shouting.

'Is Buzzle allowed to go with us tonight?' asked Little.

'Please, please, let me go,' he buzzed around Lee.

'Oh, alright. Babs, look after him closely,' Lee agreed.

'Of course, we all will,' Babs replied.

The warriors had some time before Lee came to open the door of the dome.

Everyone was so grateful to see Lee back to his happy self.

'Ember is the best thing for Lee,' Swoop mentioned.

'Very much so,' the warriors agreed.

As they all prepared for the outside world, Siggy the spindler reminded Buzzle not to wander too far.

'It is very dangerous out there,' she told Buzzle. 'You must keep close to us. Don't lose sight of any of us!'

'I will not,' promised Buzzle.

Siggy's eyes widened all eight of them, to let Buzzle know he was being watched closely.

Lee opened the door with Ember by his slide and watched the warriors disappear into the night.

'It's so exciting in Chittle Bit Lilly and… it's now my new home,' Ember said, jumping at Lee's feet.

The spindlers spun their nets.

The fledgehoggles rolled and spun.

The hodgers scooped the food.

The babbities leapt everywhere.

The squeakers yawned.

The sneasles organised everyone.

The bidgebodgers lifted all the heavy stuff.

The twitterflys kept a look-out.

The wirrels brushed everywhere clean.

What a team.

The hazers were so oblivious to the warriors that they cleaned up the mess without even being seen.

Now and then, a hazer would trip from one of the spindlers' nets or suddenly feel a strong wind around them as the fledgehoggles quickly rolled by picking up rubbish.

Most of the hazers thought it was spirits plaguing them or one of their ancestors trying to communicate.

'Why don't they pick up their own rubbish,' Buzzle asked.

'Because they are lazy. Not all of them, but some of them are and they spoil it for everyone else,' Babs told him.

'It's a good job they have us,' Buzzle replied.

Babs laughed.

Buzzle decided he was going to explore, so off he went further and further into the night. He buzzed until he realised he'd gone too far.

Whoops, where are they? he wondered, looking around.

He landed on a small flower that had closed her petals for the night. Looking around again, he didn't recognise anything.

He was getting tired so he thought he would rest for a while.

As he gazed across the street from where he was sitting, he saw a pair of eyes staring at him.

He moved slightly to the left and the eyes moved slightly to the left.

He moved slightly to the right and the eyes moved slightly to the right.

Uh oh, he thought, *I'm in trouble*.

He stood still for a few seconds, then lifted off from the flower, hovering in the air.

Slightly nervous, he moved away, back towards where the eyes followed him.

Help! he thought and buzzed harder. *Where are they?*

'Buzzle!' shouted Swoop. 'I've been looking everywhere for you. Babs told you to stay close.'

'Phew, thanks. I thought I'd lost you all,' he sighed. 'Something is following me.'

'Gypsy!' Swoop turned and shouted, 'Where have you been?'

A beautiful small black cat with piercing aqua blue eyes came into view.

'At last, I've found you again,' Gypsy purred, snuggling up to Swoop.

Swoop had landed on the path so he could get closer to her. Instantly, his feathers glowed a fluorescent deep purple and Buzzle quickly noticed.

'Swoop, you are changing colour,' he giggled.

'I know, I'm so happy to see Gypsy again,' he replied.

'Me too,' Gypsy echoed.

'Where have you been?' asked Swoop.

'I got caught up with some hazer children who, I might add, are delightful.

'I live with them sometimes, often though I'm out wandering. You know how I like to feel free,' Gypsy told them both.

Swoop had saved Gypsy when she had been hit by a car. His magic had saved her and she somehow had part of his magic.

She could heal animals in the outside world and did so elegantly.

'It's so good to see you again,' said Swoop.

'I'm pleased to see you too,' Gypsy replied.

'Who is this?' she looked at Buzzle, who was now hovering over both of them.

'This is Buzzle,' Swoop said, 'he is one of the warriors now, after Lee saved him.'

'Pleased to meet you,' Buzzle introduced himself to a fellow healer.

Gypsy laughed, 'Hi, Buzzle.'

Buzzle became a little shy and landed on Swoop.

'What are you doing, Buzzle?' Swoop said.

'Nothing,' came the reply.

'How's Lee?' Gypsy smiled.

'He's doing good, he has just healed a puppy god. We've named her Ember,' Swoop replied.

'Soon Chittle Bit Lilly will be too full for anyone else,' Gypsy said.

'Never,' replied Buzzle.

They all laughed.

'Oh, was it one of the hazers' puppy gods?' Gypsy asked.

'Yes, how did you know?' Swoop said.

'Miranda had been looking for her, she asked for my help, so here I am after hunting for two days!'

'Well she's safe in Chittle Bit Lilly now,' Swoop replied.

Gypsy had mentioned to Swoop that she was on her way back to the hazers' house and that they could all walk together.

They had a lot of catching up to do, with Buzzle ardently listening in.

Eventually they met up with the other warriors.

'Buzzle… I told you not to wander off!' Babs became angry.

'I know, I'm so sorry, I got carried away looking around.'

47

Buzzle had a sad face.

'Just don't do it again,' Wes pointed his finger. 'You had us all worried.'

'I won't, I promise,' Buzzle cheered up a little.

Gypsy said hello to everyone and went in the direction of the hazers' house.

'See you all soon,' she called back to them.

The warriors all decided not to tell Lee about Buzzle disappearing and became silent when they got to the door of the dome.

'So how did Buzzle get on?' asked Lee.

'Just fine,' Babs said looking very sternly at Buzzle, who once again was trying to buzz off somewhere.

Lee frowned and replied, 'Mmmm…'

Chapter 8

The Secret

Wes, Hog and Little were sneaking around Babs's home trying to grab a lollipop off the roof when they saw flashes of blue light shining across the windows.

'Let's take a lollipop first,' Hog snorted.

'No Hog, something's going on inside,' Wes ordered.

'Something strange,' said Little, trying to peek inside the homes.

Again, flashes of light appeared from the mound, making all of them really curious.

Inside, Babs was unaware of all of them peering through the window and watching her.

She was stamping one of her huge feet. Every now and then, blue light flashed from underneath.

'What is she doing?' Hog mumbled.

'Not sure,' Wes said. He pondered for a while and then looked at Little.

'What do you think?' he asked him.

'Maybe she's trying to dance!' answered Little.

Slowly both Wes and Hog turned to look at Little, shaking their heads.

Suddenly, Babs stamped very hard and magical blue light flew out of her foot and went around the room.

She became so excited.

'Yes…' she began, 'at last!' Wes couldn't bear it any longer so he knocked on her door.

'Are you OK?' he asked.

'Coming,' Babs replied, then caught Hog staring through the window with a lollipop in his mouth.

'Hog, you are so greedy,' Little pushed him.

Hog just grunted, pulling a face.

'Come in,' she said, then whispered to Wes, 'will tell you later.'

They all stumbled in and sat down.

'What were you doing?' Hog asked, finishing the lollipop.

'Oh, just practicing,' she said.

'For what?' said Little, being even more nosy.

'Nothing in particular, just for me,' Babs glanced over at Wes.

'OK, let's talk about business,' Wes instructed.

They often had meetings to discuss how their environmental clean-up was going. Most of the time they ended up laughing or giggling about some of the events that happened to them.

The meeting lasted for a while but nothing seemed to change.

Suddenly, there was a knock on the door, with lots of squeaky noises coming from outside.

Babs opened the door and in stumbled Itty, Bitty and Boo, followed by a dozen more squeakers, all scurrying inside.

'We've come for the meeting,' Itty squeaked.

'A bit late…' Little began.

'We are just finishing up.'

'Where's the cakes?' Bitty asked.

'Yes, where's the cakes?' Boo repeated, pulling a face.

'C'mon, you lot, it's time to clean up.' Babs ordered.

'No cakes for you!'

So they all sauntered outside to see Lee with little Ember, waiting by the door of the dome.

All the warriors were there too, waiting eagerly to do what they were good at… Cleaning rubbish.

Once they were all in the outside world, Wes questioned Babs.

'So, what were you doing?' he whispered.

'Well, I have this special magical gift which I haven't used yet and I was practicing it,' she replied, struggling to get the words out.

'Magical gift… what! Other than growing double in size, seeing in the dark and hearing for miles? Oh and jumping incredibly high?' Wes spluttered.

'What are you two whispering about?' asked Choo. 'Let's get a move on.'

Babs answered Wes, 'Yes, I can only do it on a Blue Moon and it only lasts for one minute.'

Wes kept bothering Babs the whole time to tell him what the secret was, but she promised to show him later.

Swoop was out calling in a high-pitched sound, hoping Gypsy would hear. Joop joined in a couple of times but then had to fly back to the warriors.

Eventually, Gypsy appeared and Swoop immediately asked her to find Miranda, Temica and Rikki. Once she had found them, she was to bring them to the door of the dome.

Gypsy slowly and silently made her way to the hazers' house while Swoop flew back to the warriors.

Purring very loudly, she got the attention of the three children. After getting them to come outside, she told them that they must go to the door of the dome and wait.

'What for?' asked Miranda.

'I'm not sure,' Gypsy replied.

'Let's go anyway,' Rikki began. 'It's bound to be interesting.'

Gypsy raced off into the night with the hazers following behind.

'Wait for us, kitty,' Temica said.

But it was too late; Gypsy had already gone.

They all eventually caught up just as the warriors disappeared through the door.

'I suppose we better wait here,' Temica said looking around.

'Ssshhh… yes, let's wait right here,' Miranda answered.

With all the warriors inside Chittle Bit Lilly and Lee and Ember standing by the door, Choo organised them in a line.

'If you face the entrance,' Choo began, 'you will see something really special, or so Babs has told me.'

Babs took over, telling the warriors to stay very still, wait and watch.

'So, what are we waiting for?' asked Lee.

'You'll see,' Babs smiled.

Miranda, Temica, Rikki and Gypsy were ready in the outside world while the warriors were ready in Chittle Bit Lilly.

Babs finally revealed her secret.

She has been practicing for so long that she was really, really excited.

She raised one of her back legs, stamping her foot very hard.

Then it happened!

Blue light did its work.

It slowly emerged from her foot, wound its way around the warriors, over the houses, over the star and everywhere else in Chittle Bit Lilly.

Magic took hold, making everything visible to the outside world.

Miranda, Temica, Rikki and Gypsy could see Chittle Bit Lilly.

They all stood with their eyes wide and mouths open, staring at the magical sight before them.

They could see all the warriors; Lee was waving; Ember was wagging her tail.

They could all see each other.

'Look at the houses, the star, and there's Lee with the puppy, oh how magical!'

'I can't believe it,' Miranda was so excited.

The children stood waving to them all with tears rolling down their cheeks.

Gypsy purred very loudly as Chittle Bit Lilly began to fade and was no longer visible.

'Goodbye!' they all shouted. Lee and the warriors watched as the hazers, along with Gypsy, slowly disappeared. Miranda, Temica and Rikki were still crying, gradually wiping their tears and talking about what they had just seen.

Gypsy stayed with the hazers as they made their way home, in awe of the magic that they had all experienced.

Lee also wiped the tears from his face as he remembered his time in the outside world.

Babs was delighted that her secret was out and her magical gift was shared with everyone.

'Well, that was cool,' Wes said smiling at Babs.

All the warriors agreed.

Buzzle was sniffling along with most of the warriors, so sad but also happy to have witnessed the special event.

'Maybe one day, other hazers can join us here in Chittle Bit Lilly...' Lee smiled.